T0128234

12
VARSITY
LETTERS

ED GILBERT

Order this book online at www.trafford.com
or email orders@trafford.com

Most Trafford titles are also available at major online book retailers.

Print information available on the last page.

ISBN: 978-1-4907-9628-4 (sc)
ISBN: 978-1-4907-9629-1 (hc)
ISBN: 978-1-4907-9631-4 (e)

Library of Congress Control Number: 2019909950

Trafford rev.   07/17/2019

Trafford
PUBLISHING®   www.trafford.com
North America & international
toll-free: 1 888 232 4444 (USA & Canada)
fax: 812 355 4082

CONTENTS

INTRODUCTION

I **ALMOST DID NOT** write this book. The reason was that basically it is directed toward my own athletic accomplishments and that's a sure loser by most writing standards!

However, as I glanced back at my 'four-year war' as a 'jock' at Baldwin High School where I earned a record 12 Varsity letters, I began making a few notes. Those scraps of paper eventually melded together with a few other adventures and became the story of my youthful pursuits.

Really, I wouldn't give it up for a lifetime. I thoroughly enjoyed high school sports, but somewhat ironically, beyond those and college sports, I never enjoyed the professional level.

Now, if you too had similar experiences during your school years, I invite you to read on. If not, you should pass up this book. And that would not upset me – not one winning touchdown, one last-second basket, one bases-loaded homer, or one 100-yard dash to the finish line!

Ed Gilbert

ACKNOWLEDGMENTS

FIRST AND FOREMOST, I will never forget my high school coach, Hobart (Hobey) Lewis. Fact is, I really should dedicate this short writing to Hobey, for he was not only my coach in four sports over four years, but a true friend. We hunted and fished together in addition to the hundreds of hours spent together on the football field, basketball court, and baseball and track fields.

I also must acknowledge and thank the many guys who were with me those many hours during practices and contests, winning and losing. As I'll say again somewhere in this book, "we didn't win every contest or game, but we sure had a lousy time!"

Then there is my father, Donald Gilbert, who taught me much about hunting and fishing and traveled many miles to watch me get nearly killed on the gridiron, hammered on the basketball court, and humbled at baseball and track.

My wife also offered some ideas as she proof-read various chapters, and they were invaluable.

Last, but certainly not least, I thank Gerry Vandlen, a friend who used her expertise on the computer to finalize the book for publication.

Thank you all....

Ed Gilbert

CHAPTER 1

Fun and Games

YEAH, I WAS that youngster in high school that some liked and others hated.

I won 12 Varsity Letters in 4 years of High School: I was Quarterback for the Football Team, Captain of the Basketball Team; was on the Track Team placing 2nd in Long Jump at the State Track Meet. I was Homecoming King; played the lead in the Senior Play, and in general got undeserved straight A's on my report cards. Thinking back, I even squandered chances playing second base for our Baseball Team one season. No wonder some liked me while others hated me!!!

For the "liking" part, some girls did while others shunned me due to a bad case of acne. Yes, I liked Carol, the homecoming queen, but she was one of the later ones, a year behind me in school.....

These things were going through my mind as I slowed my truck near the empty lot where Baldwin High School once stood. They'd built a new school since I was quarterback in 1952. It was a half-mile away and far over-shadowed the old two-story, drafty brick building I shared with 32 of my classmates during those formative years of fun and games....and games...

It's funny how things change almost in an instant. I'd driven my old Ford Ranger up to the hamlet of Baldwin and to fish for trout in the Pere Marquette River, but made a wrong turn off the Main Street and suddenly here I was, back in time at the "ghostly" spot of my old school.

After sitting and looking at the vacant lot for a few more minutes, I turned the Ranger around and drove back to Main Street. There I made a left turn and headed toward the old County Court House, straight up the road through town.

It was fall and the green, red and brown leaves were fluttering down in the soft breeze as I made a left turn to the west in front of the Court House and drove down the old road, past the baseball field and to the vacant field where I'd played Panther football three years. It didn't look the same. No goal posts had survived the years and shrubs and foliage had taken over the field. Just the opposite of how the new gridiron must look down by the new High School, south of town.

Suddenly my thoughts flashed back to the early 40s, when my father, who worked for the Conservation Department, was relocated from the Petoskey area to Baldwin where he took charge of the Baldwin Trout Rearing Station.

I was 9 years old when we moved, and first was captivated by all the woods and waters, where I could be able to hunt and fish nearly all year around. School and competitive sports never entered my mind at that age. Rather, I spent most of my free time in the summer by sitting on the old railroad bridge, drowning night-crawlers in front of trout that could care less; and in the fall by being indoctrinated into the hunting world by my father.

Yes, those early years came back with swiftness. As I turned to the east from downtown and drove to the old trout ponds, I recalled the day I met some of the local boys. As I said, I was drowning worms off the old railroad bridge, not having the slightest idea how to really fish or what to fish with, but a determined youngster none the less, when Tom and Jack McLenithan, near neighbors, came floating down the river on some old inner tubes.

Tom was my age and his brother Jack two years older, as I was to find out later. Jack was the "leader" type while Tom was more of a follower. They beached their tubes just below the bridge and climbed up to where I was sitting.

"You're not gonna catch any fish that way," Tom scuffed, looking my way as though I may have another series of holes in my head.

I looked at him and countered, "Oh yea? Well how do you catch 'em?"

Jack came in with, "Well, you know this here's a trout-raising station, don't you?"

"Sure. My Dad runs the place."

"So what do they feed the fish?"

"Some ground up horse meat and liver," I said in a knowing manner.

"Well," Jack said, "a lot of that feed filters through the pond and into the river where the wild trout are! That give you any ideas?"

FLASH! The lights came on suddenly and as the boys made their way back to the river and downstream,

I pulled up anchor and headed for my Dad's fish-food cooler!

The food cooler was about 10 feet square, cork-lined and had a heavy door. I pulled the door open and looked about. Inside stood a variety of 50-gallon cans, and they contained several types of fish food. There was very soft ground-up liver in several and some ground horse meat in the others.

I went to my Mom's garbage container and ferreted out an old Campbell Soup can. Returning to the cooler, I picked out some chunks of raw meat. Then I closed the heavy door and headed to the river, old fishing rod in hand and an ear-to-ear grin on my kisser!

There was one fair-sized hole in the river right behind the house. But the beauty of it was that a drain pipe emptied right from the bank into that hole, and of course that drain was from a tank in the basement where my Dad kept a few new cleaned-out food cans after they were emptied.

I placed a small chunk of horse meat on my hook and tossed it into the hole. Instantaneously, a fish gobbled that meat and within a few seconds I had a dandy rainbow trout on the bank. My, but those fish were dumb! I caught one on nearly every cast and had 15 trout within half an hour. And the limit at that time was 25 per day.

My mother was flabbergasted to say the least. At first she asked, "Eddie, were you fishing in one of the trout ponds and not in the river?"

"No," I said, and then explained that two neighbor boys had told me their fishing secret and I'd taken advantage of it.

Well, I was questioned no further, but was told to go back to the river and clean the fish.

Now then, I could have repeated that fishing day for several days and filled Mom's freezer, but she informed me not to do so, to just catch the fish as needed. What a crimp that put in my style! Here I am, with fishing heaven placed right in my hands and unable to take advantage.

Was fishing almost over for me? I thought about it and as luck would have it, my answer arrived the very next day.

I discovered an old fly rod in the work shed. It was a split bamboo rod and needed some repairs. Harold Fisher, an older fellow that worked for my Dad, tied a few feathered flies for me and oiled the reel.

So I took the contraption to the river where I whipped the waters to a frost for several days, unsuccessfully.

But on the third day along came a good ripple on my soon-to-become lagoon of happiness. I was flipping that fly over the water when a voice behind me said, "Young man, you've got to take your time when you cast a fly."

Jerking my head around, I looked up to see a tall man with a moustache staring down at me. He was grinning from ear to ear as he continued, "Let me take your rod a moment and I'll show you what I mean." So the man continued to instruct me, and I was getting the casting rhythm down quite well when my Dad walked up to us.

"Hi, Coach," Dad said to the guy. Then he turned to me and remarked, "Eddie, this is Coach Lewis from school. He coaches the various varsity teams, I believe."

"Just football, basketball, track and baseball," laughed Coach Lewis. Then he sort of grunted out, "The school can't afford any more coaches, so I fumbled my way through an interview and they hired me."

"Eddie," my Dad said, "Mr. Lewis is only kidding. He is a fine coach from what I hear. He knows his stuff and the kids all admire him. He's had some good teams, too."

"Thank you, Mr. Gilbert," Coach Lewis remarked, "and say, keep this young man flinging flies with his right arm and someday I'll make him into a good strong-armed quarterback."

What's a quarterback, I thought!

Well, I didn't think about Coach Lewis much as the months and years rolled by, but suddenly I found myself a freshman in high school. Little did I know what was in store for me over the next four years – it would be like a 4-year war.

CHAPTER 2

From Fishing to Football

BALDWIN HIGH SCHOOL had never fielded a football team until the year I showed up as a freshman — all 130 pounds of me!

But I wasn't the only freshman who made the scene. Along came Ivan Ives, Tom McLenithan, Bill Ayers, Don Pequette, Jack Bramer, Clarence Bitely, Judd Copeland, Sam Avery, and several other teammates whose names I've long forgotten.

We had no practice facility but used a vacant field, a good walk from school. Fact is, we often referred to it as our "turkey patch."

Now, I knew nothing really about the game of football, but as I watched the older boys working out and running plays I decided quarterback was where I wanted to play. In practice I found that I could punt the ball quite accurately, with a spiral and with some distance. Coach Lewis noticed it too, and as a freshman I became our team's punter.

But there was a problem. We didn't have a strong line and since at the time there was no rule about creaming the punter, I got roughed up badly and often. Fortunately, however, we weren't playing the Green Bay Packers, but some of our own guys, so I came through the first few practices relatively unscathed....but not totally. When hit in the head area, we had little protection and it seemed as though my head was a target. We wore simple leather helmets and no face masks, as any other head protection just didn't exist.

I'd been throwing the ball a lot and accurately and Coach Lewis noticed that as well.

Sure, I wanted to be a quarterback, but a big kid named Bob Sizor, a senior, seemed to want that position also. But Sizor had a problem. His eyesight was poor and he didn't pass or lateral the ball with accuracy.

Then it happened – during practice, Sizor got the ball out of the T-formation and turned to lateral the ball to the kid who was coming around to skirt the right side. I saw it coming, so from my safety position I ran between the two of them, intercepting the ball and running it for a touchdown, with Bob running after me and swearing, "You little s.o.b! I'll get you, etc., etc.!"

The next day I was inserted as quarterback and Coach Lewis added a few pass plays. Things went well at the practice, even though I got some strange or even bitter looks from some of the older boys. Bob Sizor quit the team.

Following a few evenings of practice, I was walking home with a neighbor, Sam Avery, and fired a question at him. "Bob is really mad at me, isn't he?"

"Mad? No, he's fuming. You made a fool of him during practice and he couldn't take it."

"Well, I guess I can't blame him, at that."

I mentioned to my Dad what had happened. "Well," he said, "Bob wasn't a good leader anyway, and in the end he would probably have hurt the team." He said Bob was just a bully at heart, and he proved it.

I grabbed my fly rod when I got home and headed down stream for some fishing. There was a little daylight left and I was whipping the waters to a froth when Coach Lewis walked up behind me, nearly losing an ear from my fly casting as he dodged and recanted, "Hey, Eddie, I'd like to talk for a minute, if we can do that."

"Now look," Coach began as I leaned my fly rod against a tree and joined him, taking a seat on the bank, "I've done something here that I probably shouldn't do and never have before."

He paused and thought a moment before continuing. "You are very young, but talented for your age, and I've put you at a position on our team that can be causing you problems. Quarterback is a ...."

"What problem?" I entreated.

"Quarterback is the leadership position on any football team and some older guys will resent taking orders from someone much younger," Coach answered.

"I've already experienced some of that," I replied, "but not much. I guess I can handle it. The plays I call are yours, anyway."

"Well, it can be serious, so I want you to know what to expect. This is our first year as a team and in the league. It will probably be a couple of years before we can make a run at the league championship. By then you and others on the team will be much more experienced. In the meantime, and I hate saying it, you can expect to take a beating in some of our league games."

"Who's in our league?" I asked as I glanced up questioningly.

"Let's see….There is Newaygo, White Cloud, Grant, Hesperia, Ravenna, and Kent City," Coach replied. "But I've already scheduled one non-league scrimmage. That will be up at Cadillac, and they are Class B, while we're really a small Class D." He paused, and then said, "We're going up to play them next Friday."

"Wow!" I found myself saying under my breath. "That could get dangerous, couldn't it?"

Then, as though I wasn't really thinking of a problem, "It's really only a practice session, though, right?"

"Well, yes." He looked at me with a little concern, and then continued, "You know there aren't enough good players on our team now to have an offense and a separate defense, so some of you will be going both ways. You will, but you'll be at the safety position on defense. On offense you'll start at quarterback."

I merely looked at him, expecting Coach to continue. He did.

"I didn't want our first year on offense to be too confusing and that's why I only passed out 12 plays: four passing and eight running plays. You know them and have been handing the ball off well and passing fast and with accuracy. I'll be sending in some of the plays by alternating the ends, Jack and Bill. When they don't alternate in, you'll be on your own to call the play."

I didn't answer right away. For the most part, I was thinking about those ends, Jack and Bill. Both were long, lean and lanky and again, both were freshmen along with me. Jack had great hands, but Bill had nearly as bad eyesight as had Sizor, and I had to hit him in stride and right on the numbers for him to grab the football.

However, when Bill did catch it, he had blazing speed and could be a real threat.

"I know it will be important," I finally said, "to call the right plays on time in the huddle and that will depend on the situation we're at on the field. I've been reading some books on football and trying to figure all that out."

"You and I will get together on all that and a few more things before we practice against Cadillac," Coach replied with a grin. "See you in school Monday. I'd better get back to my happy home and the wife and two daughters." With that he walked back up and along the stream toward the fishing site.

He'd mentioned his wife and daughters, and although I knew little of them, I knew she was about 5-feet tall while he was about 6'5". They'd made a great couple at one of the school's Saturday night dances they'd chaperoned. The daughters were six and four years old and they all lived in a refurbished Quonset hut on the south end of town.

Coach told us one day in his history class how he'd been in Germany with General Patten during the recent War. When he touched on the subject during any class, we all jumped on him to tell us more. And he would do so....Funny, Coach turned only 28 years old that year, but to us players, he was like "the old man".

It was getting dark and I grabbed up my fly rod and walked slowly down river toward home. It was getting colder and the red and brown leaves were flying in the breeze around me. Somehow, I really felt good.

CHAPTER 3

Practice "Schmackist!"

THE TEAM TOOK a school bus from Baldwin up to Cadillac, with Coach at the wheel. It seemed like a fine outing and everyone was in a jovial mood.

That abruptly changed once we took to the football field. The whole setting was different.

The school was huge and the playing field was immaculate, while ours back home somewhat resembled an over-grown turkey patch and was located a good half mile from our old brick school house.

We took to our sideline and I glanced over the field at what seemed like 50 players, all dressed in their finest. It was already demoralizing and as I looked around at our 23 players in our blue and gold attire, it seemed even worse.

We kicked off following the coin toss, and Cadillac had a little speedster that tore up the sideline to our 40-yard line. They ran a single-wing offense, and on their first play the fullback took a direct snap from center. He was well on 6-feet tall, over 200 pounds, and tore through our line and directly at my safety position. I had no choice. I could lie down or attempt a tackle. It was obvious that he intended to run right through me, so at the last moment I fell backwards and reached out my right hand.

It was just enough. I caught him by a shoe and he fell forward going full tilt. The ball was under him and his wind went out with a gush. The schoolboy referee rushed out, his whistle blasting, and their Coach and several players helped the fullback to their sidelines. He didn't reappear for another two series of plays, but he wasn't that critical to their offense as they scored on their next two possessions.

For our team, it was like David against Goliath. We couldn't run against their huge line, so what progress we did make was through the air.

In our third possession I called for Jack on a square out from right end. The play was simply 10-right end. Jack took two strides down field and cut for the flat, where I met him with the pass. The play netted a good five yards!

Back in the huddle I glanced about and quickly called the same play "10-right end, on one – break!" We ran it again and it got us a first down inside their 20-yard line. We repeated it two more times; then I called for 10-left end. Bill was wide open at the 10-yard line. I hit him on his "60", and he walked into the end zone!

Cadillac's coach was furious with his defense and stormed about on their sidelines.

Following that bit of frivolity, each side took turns returning kick-offs.

Finally it was clear we couldn't have beaten them in a real game, as most of our players were pretty well beat up or somewhat demoralized.

Back aboard the bus and before he took the wheel, Coach got our attention. "Boys," he began, "you all played remarkably well. They have a tough team and they out-weighed us by a bunch. For your first competition I think you played great. But really, the idea to have practice against them was to see where our weak points and strengths are so we can work on those this coming week." He paused and then said, "We're going down to Newaygo next Friday afternoon for our first game!"

We worked on blocking and tackling on Monday through Thursday, but also honed some of our offensive plays. We ran a simple offense, the straight T-formation with me under Horner our center, Hood at left halfback, Dobrey at right halfback and Bitely at fullback.

Most of our plays were designed to go through the 2 or 3-hole, right or left of center. I would take the center snap, pivot and either hand the ball off to Hood or Dobrey, to the hole right or left, or fake the hand-off and drop back to pass, or even lateral the ball to Bitely the fullback who would look for an opening and take off. The line blocking assignments were also simple and, of course, depended on who would end up with the ball.

Yes, it was a simple offense, but for a first-year team it could be effective, provided of course everyone did his job, whether blocking or running.

CHAPTER 4

Our First Season of Football

NEWAYGO WAS A Class C school and had been in our league, the "North Central Athletic Association (NCAA)" for several years. All our league teams were within a two-hour drive from Baldwin, and Newaygo was less than an hour away.

This time we had a regular bus driver while Coach spent much of the trip ambling up and down the aisle as he offered advice or remarks. He had little to say to me then, most of it being said already on the bank of the Pere Marquette River earlier on.

We won the coin toss and elected to receive the ball per Coach's instructions. Also, he gave me the first three plays to call just before kick-off, so there wasn't a lot of thinking to do. The first two were 32 right and 22 left, meaning Dobrey through the right side 2-hole and Hood through the left side 2-hole.

Neither play went for more than 2 yards and it was suddenly third down and 6 yards to go for a first down. The third play Coach called was a look-in pass to Dobrey who took three strides through the line and angled to his left. The ball hit him squarely in the chest and bounced away, incomplete.

On fourth down I dropped back 15 yards and punted. It wasn't an exceptionally good kick, and their receiver grabbed the ball in full stride, wove his way through our defense, and ended up standing in the end zone with the first touchdown.

But there were others as we ended up on the short end of that game, 30-13.

Our ensuing three games were experiences. We'd lost that first one to Newaygo, then others to Grant and White Cloud. But our fourth game came against Kent City, and I scored on a one-yard run to make the score 6-6 with only a few seconds left on the clock.

Our Coach was signaling me to run for the extra point, but I pretended not to hear him and knelt down to receive the ball. I placed it on the ground and let Judd Copeland kick it. The ball went up, hit the cross bar and bounced over. It was our first win, 7-6.

Hesperia and Ravenna were the final line-up that first season, and although we were getting better with each game, we lost to Hesperia 20-14 and barely squeaked by Ravenna 14-13.

That's how I won my first of 12 Varsity Letters at Baldwin High School.

Coach was ecstatic that we won two games in our initial season and told us so at a dinner put on by our parents. He closed our first football season by remarking, "I'm proud of these young men, proud of how they matured, and very proud of our first season."

He paused then and his final remark of the evening was, "Now it's on to basketball. Our first game will be in just three weeks, and I have no idea how that's going to come out. However, I'll see many of you boys on the basketball court Monday afternoon after school....Get some rest in the meantime. I have a feeling we're going to have a good basketball season."

The first Baldwin football team - 1948

CHAPTER 5

Making the Varsity Basketball Team and a Bow Hunt

HERBIE, MARV AND Pete were all seniors this year. They made up most of the power on our basketball team.

Baldwin had a team in the NCAA for seven years already. We played the same schools as in football, and were near the 70% mark on wins the year before. Both of the starting guards had graduated the year before, however, and that accounted for two weak spots in the starting five.

I went out for the team, but as a freshman it soon became obvious that I hadn't much of a chance of cracking that line-up. I was like a bush in a forest of tall trees.

Meanwhile, Coach's mind had been spinning and he organized a freshman team, comprised of most of the frosh who had played on the initial football team. Well, we could at least get some experience, he figured.

We did. Since our school wasn't really laid out to field a Junior Varsity (J.V.) team, he pitted us anyway against the NCAA JV's in our league. We won our first four games, home and away, and looked pretty sharp in the bright gold uniforms some of the parents had chipped in to purchase.

Basketball seemed to come easy for me and I was scoring over 15 points per game from the right guard slot during those first games.

Coach noticed it too and one Saturday afternoon he showed up in my yard with one of the Varsity players. They unloaded and put up a used basketball backboard in the side yard of my home. I thanked him, my Dad thanked him, my mother thanked him, and all but my older sister thanked him!

"There," Coach said. "Now you can get in a lot more practice." He turned about and then asked, "Say, Eddie, do you have a bow? It's almost deer season for bow and arrow hunters. We can hunt together sometime."

So I told Coach I had an old Cedarquest metal bow, but wasn't very proficient with it.

"Doesn't matter," he replied. "Next weekend we'll give it a try---say, Saturday morning?"

"Okay," I said. Then, retrieving my basketball from my bedroom, I shot hoops until it was too dark to see the rim.

Between then and Saturday I pulled my bow and shot several times, using my old wooden arrows. I wasn't good and the bow had too much poundage for me. There seemed no way I could hold it back and release it accurately without setting up a quiver. Oh, but that didn't matter; I was just thinking of the hunt itself.

Coach arrived at my house about 6 a.m. the Saturday we were to hunt and we motored down to about two miles south of Newaygo to his brother's house. From there we walked about a mile into the woods and set up in the brush on either side of a deer runway.

About a half hour later a buck and doe ran in between us and their hoofs pounded on up the runway. I tried to pull back my bow, but got it back late, so never loosed an arrow. Later, Coach said he didn't get an arrow off either as the deer ran straight between us and he thought it would have been a dangerous shot in my direction. Yes, I agreed.

I thanked him for that hunt several times and insisted we try it again the following week. We did and that too wasn't a successful hunt.

However, that was but a small ripple on my lagoon of happiness that day as on the way home we stopped at a doughnut shop and Coach remarked, "Eddie, I'm going to move you up to the Varsity team this week…. you'll be playing right guard with Whitey Dobrey at left guard. I think you two will work well together and you both can not only shoot well but can pass the ball inside to the big guys. Now, I know you can shoot the ball, you're averaging at least 15 points per game, but I'd like you to look to pass it before taking shots. We'll need teamwork, just like back in our football season. And once again, you are only a freshman while our entire Varsity is now made up of juniors and seniors." He paused a moment as though to let that sink in, and then, "You know what it was like when you broke in at quarterback on the football team. You had some items to overcome at the hands of a few older boys. I just want you to know that the same can happen, but if you do your best you'll overcome any antagonism."

I sat there during Coach's talk, drinking milk and trying not to choke on a couple of chocolate doughnuts, but inside I was as happy as a pig wallowing in mud. I needed to get home and spring this new development on my parents. Then I'd shoot some hoops for an hour or so and close the day by whipping the waters to a froth fly-fishing the Pere Marquette River.

It turned out to be pretty good fishing that evening. Below me in a deep hole a large brown trout was rising to suck something off the top of the water. I reached into my pack of flies and pulled out a "mousie". It was a fuzzy fly, about the size of a small mouse, and one of the best lures ever tied by local business woman, Josephine (Joe) Sedlecky of Ed's Sport Shop in Baldwin.

I walked in above the fishing hole and let out the fly line, letting the lure get in the vicinity of where that brown trout was rising. Suddenly there was a gigantic splash as the brownie inhaled that fly. And when it did, I was looking at a trout that would scale in least at15 pounds!!! I reared back, but I knew in an instant that my fly leader wouldn't hold that monster. I'd have needed a rope or chalk line!

Then the fish made a run downstream, snapping my line as though it were thread.

"Well now," I said to myself as I got to shore and walked back home, "I'll bet you're halfway back to Lake Michigan by now. But you know what? I don't care. I just made the Varsity Basketball Team."

CHAPTER 6

Center Jump and a Big Buck!

JUST AS HE had for football, Coach fashioned a fairly simple offense and defense. Our offense had both guards with alternating forwards cutting to the hoop or a pass in to Ayers at center. We played a zone defense with the guards out front and the forwards and center inside. At the time there were no rules about how long one could stay in the hoop zone. Marvin set up shop there.

Three upper classmen, Bill, Jack and Pete, were inside and were all fairly tall. Marvin at center was about 6'4." Practice went well. We suited up 11 boys for the team and Coach had us 5 starters run plays against the others, even letting them use 6 on defense on occasion.

Our practice sessions ran from 3:30 to 5:00 every afternoon and the usual criteria included racing up and down the court, dodging chairs while we dribbled the ball, pausing, position shooting, guarding details and shooting free throws. Then after a brief scrimmage, we hit the shower.

We didn't have a basketball court at the school but used one in downtown Baldwin for practice and games. Coach encouraged us to run from the school to practice, and it did help in conditioning. After all, basketball is a running game and you are constantly on the move. You don't get easily winded or you can't play the game, it's that simple.

By this week the team had already played six games, losing three and winning three. But we played each team twice, once on their court and the other at home. We won all of our home games and lost three played on the other team's court. I don't know how others saw it then, but it was clear to me that every home team had an advantage. That included us, from the referees to the crowd which was so close to all the courts that it seemed to loom over us. It was loud but exciting and the refs had to be graded by the home school after each game, so this too was a situation. But when play actually began, I found that less and less I heard the noise and was into the game itself. As for the referees, they were simply like other players on court.

The first varsity game for me was at home against Newaygo. As the center jump was to start, I edged down court a few steps and Bill went up high at center, slapping the ball down the court in my direction. I grabbed the ball in full stride with no defender near me, dribbled several times and laid it in. The home crowd was loud and shouted my name. I was hooked on the game of basketball forever!

We won that game by a close score of 61-59. Bill and I combined for 43 of those points, and in a way that presented a problem. Our other players had fed us the ball constantly, to Bill for an inside shot and to me for outside one-handed set shots. They'd taken but a few shots themselves and Coach addressed that during the following practice...

"When you've got a good open shot, take it," he addressed the others. He grinned then. "No, I don't mean from center court or from under the other basket, just practice your open shots, and when one comes, take it." Then he laughed wickedly. "Only thing is, you'd better make it!"

The weekend following my first varsity game was the opening of the firearms deer season in Michigan. Dad figured I didn't need a rifle yet, but he let me carry my Mom's 20-gauge Mossberg shotgun with slugs.

We went up in the hills southeast of Wolf Lake and he put me in a spot on a runway and walked on up the trail. I'd sat down on a fallen tree and kept still and quiet for about an hour when several shots rang out to the west. I faced that direction and waited. Suddenly a 6-point buck ran up to within about 15 yards of me, stopped and simply stood their broadside.

I clicked the safety off, aimed at the heart area of the deer and fired. I figured at best the deer would run off and I'd need to follow it, but that wasn't the case. The buck simply fell over, dead!

I had my first deer at age 14 and was pleased as punch. "Wow," I thought. "This is simple." Then my father came running, congratulated me, and we dressed out the deer and hauled it back to the fender of his Pontiac and went home.

It was great, but more success followed. The next day, already having my deer, I tagged along with Dad and didn't carry a gun. We hunted atop one side of an old gravel pit, and suddenly Dad raised his old Springfield .06, adjusted the rear sight for distance, and aimed off across the pit. It must have been more than

600 yards to where I fully noticed the buck, standing on the opposite ridge and facing us.

Dad's rifle barked and the deer disappeared.

"Don't be in a hurry," Dad remarked. "We'll walk over there and see if there's any blood or sign of a hit."

It took perhaps 15 minutes to navigate that old gravel pit and climb up the other side, but when we reached the top, there laid his deer, a 10-point beauty.

"What a shot," I remarked. "You're good, Dad." Then I remembered that Dad had been a marksman back in the First World War. He'd been hit in the left shoulder by a German machine gunner and carried a metal plate in that shoulder ever since.

What a weekend of hunting we'd had together in Michigan's woods. (It almost made me forget that another basketball game was coming up on Friday and several more to follow over the next few weeks.])

It was ironic, I guess, but we closed that basketball season by winning half of our games and losing the other half, again. With seven teams in our NCAA league, including ours, it meant six wins and six losses.

But we still had Tournament action. We played the games over at Big Rapids in a much larger gym, and we lost in our second game, to Leroy. But we'd had a good season and were all looking forward to the following season, except for the seniors who'd played their last basketball game. I felt sorry for them and wondered what next season would be like without them.

CHAPTER 7

Winter Sports

IT WAS WINTERTIME in Michigan, and in many places, the snow was up to, what Dad used to call 'my stacking swivel'. That wasn't unusual, but with basketball season ended, it was time to get on with whatever was available.

We had a few hills in the woods across the river behind our house. So I thought about skiing, and one day mentioned it to one of Dad's employee's, old 'Doc' Fisher. A few days later he presented me with a set of skis he'd fashioned himself. They had no boot tie-downs except pieces of rubber inner tubes nailed to the sides, just enough to keep the feet from slipping off.

Later on in years I did learn to ski quite well, but at that earlier time I walked up those hills and came back down on the skis, falling often and even crashing into a few trees. I still have some scars!

Then one young friend and neighbor boy, Sam Avery, got me into ice hockey. There were several large ponds within a short walk of my house. Sam, along with the McLenithan brothers, Jack and Tom, all had ice skates. I sort of begged Mom for skates, and behold! a pair of hockey skates magically appeared under the tree that Christmas.

Organized school-team hockey wasn't even considered back then, at least in our part of the country, so hockey sticks and pucks simply weren't available.

Not to matter, we cut branches from trees to fashion clubs and tied a stone inside a sock for a puck. Now, if you've never been hit by a large club or even a stone traveling about 60 miles per hour, you simply haven't lived!

Oh, but you felt a hero when someone clubbed you in the back or on the head or you caught a stone alongside an ear.

Well now, Sam and I normally paired off against Jack and Tom. Sam, a multiple-position player on our football team, was big and dangerous. So we usually won.

Then one day, and quite unexpectedly, another winter past-time reared its head. While skating along one day on a nearby backwater, on ice that was clear as glass, I spotted a large bass. I stood right over it and it didn't move, so I whacked the ice with my skates. It only moved about a foot and stopped. It was a whopper!

That was proof enough that this fish could be mine. I removed my skates and raced home, where I discovered Doc Fisher in the basement cleaning out some horsemeat cans. I told Doc what I'd seen and he took me to the repair garage, where he reached up on the wall and retrieved an ancient casting rod. Then he motioned to me to get an axe from a corner, told me to be careful, and went back to work.

I took up the axe and fishing rod and went back to the backwater where I'd seen the fish. It was still there, but at the first whack on the ice to make a hole, it sped off through the stumps that popped up like mushrooms all over that backwater.

Being a little perturbed, I started to walk off and slipped down, flat on my back. That double-bladed axe flew in the air, came down beside me, and the end of it hit squarely on the middle finger of my right hand.

Blood gushed everywhere and I stumbled home, sick to my stomach. Mom took me to Doc Mullenberg on Baldwin's west side and he sewed it up, saying I'd be all right but would lose that fingernail eventually. He told me it had been good that one of the axe's sharp edges hadn't come down on my hand. If so, I could have lost some fingers.

I thought about that, but I had another thought as well. And it wasn't pleasant. I was thinking about football and basketball and how such could affect my throwing or even handling the ball. As soon as I could, I grabbed either my football or basketball and began to practice. Soon the pain faded as I could handle them quite well.

CHAPTER 8

Spring Games

OF COURSE, IN the fall and winter we had football and basketball. Then along came spring and Baldwin High School fielded a baseball team along with a track team.

My Dad, a long-time Detroit Tigers fan, loved baseball and wanted me to try out for the team.

A couple of years later, circumstances were such that I did play some baseball, but not in my freshman year. I liked running, jumping and things that kept me moving, not hanging around a base or watching grass grow in an outfield.

I found that I could high jump, long jump and run fairly fast, so that's where I hung my hat.

For the running, I ran the 100-yard dash and was a mid-distance runner in the 880 relay. I was better at the running broad (long) jump and practiced that until I could reach nearly 17 feet. The high jump was also a favorite, but as a freshman, I was able to only reach 5'2", not high enough to compete with upper classmen.

That freshman year on the track squad was an experience that kept me in good physical condition, but as I said, competing with others, especially those league foes we faced, was almost impossible.

Why did I make the track team at all as a freshman? I guess it was really because of the size of our school. For example, there were only 33 kids in our freshman class and about 125 in our entire high school. Coach needed bodies, and I was willing. Besides, that's where I was to earn the third of my 12 Varsity letters.

Our track squad held its own regular meets, but the real fun came when our Conference meet was held at White Cloud that spring. I got my first medals there. Our 440 team came in third, and I got a second place in the high jump.

The high jump was different back then. Just as in football, where we had those flat leather helmets rather than those later with fancy face guards, you took the high jump with one foot over first and you kicked your heel up on the other foot to clear the bar and hopefully make it over.

In later years, the "Fosbery Flop" came along, where one could leap over head first and kick both feet up. It became a lot easier than the old "Western-roll" and new heights made the record books in high schools and colleges all over the country.

As spring ended and my freshman year as well, I again found time to toss hoops in my yard. And good old Doc Fisher rigged up a tire on a swing so I could practice throwing a football through the center. The only problem was, I had but one football. Then one day Coach dropped in to visit, saw what I was doing, and left again to show up soon with five more footballs he'd taken from a gym locker.

The last Saturday of April has been the opening of the general trout season in Michigan for as long as I can remember. That was a day I always looked forward to, and still do. I've made a pilgrimage to the Pere Marquette River for that opening day every year since, save for the years when I was with the Marines in the Korean War.

It of course heralded the beginning of summer fishing, and I was like the proverbial kid in a candy store. I prepared for it with gusto!

On the opening evening I was by the river at midnight, waiting for someone to yell out, "Twelve o'clock!" When someone did, the air was filled with lines and bait from dozens of fishermen along the banks. This was of course soon followed by shouts of "Hey! You've snagged my line!" and in some cases complete chaos ensued.

I soon learned to open the season either up or downstream from the maddening crowd, away from parked cars, bridges or dams. That way I could even catch fish. One thing I did all those years ago on opening morning of trout season was to fish with friends. Two of those friends were of course the neighbor boys I'd met along the river after we first arrived at Baldwin, Tom and Jack McLenithan.

But that opening morning my Mom Beryl decided to make a large batch of chili and suggested that we three boys set up a card table by the river and sell it at 25 cents a bowl. She even gave us some bowls and spoons, so about noon that opening morning we set up shop.

The enterprise went so well that we made enough money to not only pay Mom back but to purchase a tent and some camping supplies for summer camp-outs.

And camp we did, mostly along the Middle Branch of the Pere Marquette River, where we'd camp on weekends. There, we'd put "set-lines" in the river in the evening, which was strictly illegal of course, and enjoyed a great Sunday morning breakfast of brown and rainbow trout. It was a great summer, and ended too soon.

CHAPTER 9

A Difficult Football Season

AS MY SOPHOMORE year approached, I received a call from Coach. I was to get my physical for football.

As it turned out, he'd called about 25 others as well and we took physicals at Doc Mullenberg's office in late August. It was an opportunity to meet up with some of the players I hadn't seen all summer, and also to notice that, obviously, three seniors from last year were no longer around and there were several freshman wannabees as well.

I thought my physical went well. However, that evening following dinner, my Dad said he'd had a call from the doctor that afternoon.

"Eddie, the doctor says you have a slight heart murmur and he told me you shouldn't play football right away. He said he wanted to check you again in a few weeks, however, as things could change for the better."

I was devastated to say the least, and fumed about the house that evening and most of the following day.

The team was depending on me to play. I was sure of that. Who would be starting as quarterback? Who could pass well and also punt the ball? Who knew the plays and how to call them as well as I did? Frankly, I could think of no answers and found myself wallowing in self-pity.

But a car suddenly pulled into the yard and it was Coach. I ran out and met him in the driveway.

"Coach, did you speak to the doctor?" I asked quickly before he could hardly exit his car.

Coach got out and stood for a moment with the car door open. Then he offered in a deliberative tone, "Yes, Dr. Mullenberg called me and his concern was for you. He said he hated to do it, but that a heart murmur could be serious and that you should go easy in practice and perhaps not even play in the first couple of games. Maybe after that…."

"I'm not sure about what I should really do," I interrupted. "If I can't play, well…"

"All you need to do is take it easy during practice to begin with, and our first game isn't for another three weeks." He paused briefly, and then continued, "But what you can also do is give me a hand at coaching one or two boys. That will be for someone to fill in at quarterback until you can play.

My mind ran through a possible lineup and I said, "I don't know. That'll be tough. I'm really not sure of anyone right now. We may have a talented freshman or two coming on the team, but all the regulars? Well, I'm not sure."

Coach leaned back on his car and brought a hand up to his chin. Then he looked squarely at me and said, "Eddie, you are smart enough to help, so I'm asking you to keep thinking your position over and tell me if any of the other boys come to mind. Also, I want you to attend all practice sessions, but with no competitive action until things change. Okay?"

I nodded, and with that Coach waved a good-bye to Dad, who was standing in the kitchen doorway, and returned to his car.

Well, all the 'maybe's' or 'perhaps in a couple of weeks' remarks didn't help. I was non-plussed and wanted to play.

I moped around for a few days and threw some footballs through the swinging tire at the old oak tree. Then my thoughts slowly turned to what Coach Lewis had asked of me. "Look for someone to fill in at quarterback until you can play," he'd said, or really had 'asked' of me.

I hadn't seen any freshman other than those who'd showed up for physicals with the rest of us, but those came to mind and I wandered through the possibilities.

There was John Chapel, who was quite small. Then there was Lee Cabin, who was very smart and built like an athlete. Ivan Ivers also came to mind. He was small but extremely wiry and stronger, perhaps better on the defensive or offensive line somewhere. But, I couldn't be sure, never seeing any of them around or even near a football.

The day prior to our first scheduled practice I approached Coach, following the History Class he taught.

"Coach," I said when the room had cleared, "I've thought of one possibility for quarterback. He happens to be a freshman, Lee Cabin, but I think I can work with him."

Coach Lewis' face lit up. "Good, Eddie, I want you to take him aside and work with him on the plays and how to handle the physical movements at quarterback for those plays. I spotted him too, and he may help us."

So began my sophomore year of football at Baldwin High School....on the sidelines.

CHAPTER 10

Potpourri for the Season

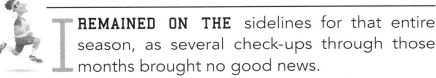

I **REMAINED ON THE** sidelines for that entire season, as several check-ups through those months brought no good news.

Meanwhile, I worked with the coach to help the team. But we had too few experienced players and lost our first four games. Rather than playing each team twice as in basketball, we played each team only once in football. I guess that was a good thing, particularly for this season. It was short and we fielded an inexperienced roster of players.

Asked about our ongoing season, one of our players offered that old remark, "Well, we're not winning any games, but we're sure having a lousy time."

While my lost football season was ongoing I turned a year older, and I guess I discovered girls, or perhaps it was vice versa. I'm not certain, but one older girl and two younger ones certainly seemed interested. One of the younger ones kept coming down to our house by the river nearly every evening, where she sat by the river bank and opened a sandwich. She kept looking my way with a predatory gleam in her eyes, but I tried to remain uninterested. It was difficult as I was feeling my age.

Our town had an ice house just off the main drag, and Sam and I would sometimes entice girls to join us in our 'secret spot'. Of course the object wasn't to 'cool them off"! Just the reverse, so our ploys never worked. Not once, dang it!

The girl I really got interested in was a year younger than me and in her freshman year. She was a cheerleader, very intelligent, and had many of the boys sniffing around her. I finally decided to leave her alone and get back to the remaining two games of our football season.

Both games were away, at Hesperia and Ravenna. Hesperia should go in our winning column, which wasn't even established yet this season, but Ravenna had been our first ever win in last year's first season. We'd won it by a single point, 7-6, and we knew they'd be laying for revenge. And we did win over Ravenna, 13-7, thanks to some aggressive defensive play. I was signaling in plays to Lee at quarterback, and he'd learned as the season progressed, but wasn't as sharp as he needed to be.

The team performed better against Ravenna however, where Whitey scored twice from his right halfback position, and Lee ran one in as a quarterback sneak from the three-yard line. We won 20-13 and Coach was elated.

On the bus back home, Coach remarked, "Boys, I'm proud of you. You came back from a lopsided beginning of the season to win two very important games and set us up for a great beginning next year....Now, with our football season behind us, we've got to look forward to playing basketball. That season begins in three weeks, so we're going to start practice next Friday afternoon. I expect to see some of you there."

His last remark rang in my ears for the remainder of the ride home, for I had a Monday appointment with Dr. Mullenberg, where he'd check to see if I could play basketball.

That Saturday we had a snowstorm that dropped nearly a foot of white stuff. Following shoveling chores and a stint at helping Dad chop some holes in the frozen ponds so he and Harold could feed about 40,000 fish, I shot hoops in the snow for an hour, concentrating on free throws and a new shot I was developing.

A few years before, I'd made a small ball out of several rocks and practiced shooting right-handed hook shots into a basket in our basement. I ran to the right and launched the ball from over and behind my head. I got so I could hit that basket nearly every time.

So, on this day in the snow, I ran to my right and launched the basketball over and behind my head. It went in the hoop, never touching the rim. Ah ha!, I thought, this could fit my game. I played right guard anyway, and a right hook from the corner would be impossible for the opposition to guard. I practiced that hook shot for another hour.

It was all well and good, but now I could look forward to Monday's visit at the doctor's office. It would be a pivotal moment in my high school years.

CHAPTER 11

"Good to Go" and
A Fishing Experience

I WALKED INTO THE Doctor's office that Monday morning with apprehension all over me. Then I waltzed my way out! Dr. Mullenberg had poked and prodded me front and back, and listened intently to my heart and lung areas. Finally, he removed the stethoscope from his ears and gave me a smile.

"You're good to go," was all he said.

"I can play basketball this season?" I shot back.

"I don't know, can you?" he countered with a grin.

"You bet I can!" I shouted as I headed for the door.

I approached Coach in the hallway that afternoon. "Doc says I can play basketball," I said, barely able to keep my feet on the ground.

Coach Lewis slapped me on the back so hard I nearly fell down. "Great, Eddie. And that will mean you'll be able to run track next year and play football in the fall as well?"

"I guess so. Doc said I had no problem any longer and it likely would not come back."

"Great!" he mused aloud as he strolled off. "See you this afternoon on the basketball court!"

And so it was. We had the usual practice sessions, every afternoon Monday through Friday, and Coach even scheduled a couple of non-league games prior to our Conference schedule.

We won over Custer by a lopsided score of 82-37 and I made 32 points from the right corner of the court. Then we ran over Luther in the same fashion. Looking back, I guess neither game was competitive as both schools had fewer enrollments than Baldwin.

Then, just prior to our league's first game, and when trout fishing was about to close for the season, something happened that made fishing eventually more important than high school sports.

On a Saturday evening I was fly-fishing, or that's what I thought I was doing, when an older gentleman in very expensive-looking fishing attire walked up to me.

I had just successfully caught an overhead branch with a 'buck tail' fly and he reached up and rescued it for me as he remarked, "Looks like you could use a lesson or two on fly-fishing, eh, young man?"

With that, he gently removed my fly rod from my hand and put his own in my other hand. It was a spit-bamboo rod with a fly reel that must have come from heaven!

For the next hour, until darkness came on us, this old man gave me instructions in fly-fishing. He showed me 10-to-2 o'clock casting method and made me practice it until I could fling the fly just about where I wanted it to land on the water, or occasionally in a tree!

The old man asked, as we prepared to close the session, "You're Don Gilbert's son, aren't you?"

I answered with a "yes, sir," as he disappeared downstream toward a fishing site.

Of course I told my father what happened and he told me he thought he knew the man from somewhere as he smiled a sort of knowing smile.

I thought little more of the incident and went about school and basketball practice in the next week. But on Saturday there came a large package to our door. It was addressed to me.

Inside the package was a case that contained a new split-bamboo fly rod, a fly reel, numerous feathers and small pieces of animal pelts and a tying vice, along with a book entitled, *"How to Tie Flies."* The package had an inscription on it that read, "Richardson Tackle Company, Chicago."

Somewhat bewildered, I turned to Dad. "Why did I receive this?"

My Father replied, "That came from the man who gave you fly-fishing lessons last week. His name is Richardson and he's the owner of a tackle company. He has come up here fishing during many a year and he told me what he was going to send you. He is a fine gentleman."

I wrote a letter thanking Mr. Richardson and began tying flies.

CHAPTER 12

Back to the Court, Man-to-Man

THIS WAS MY sophomore year to play basketball for Baldwin High School and we were to play two games against each team, at home and away. We had played them the year before, so we knew the usual suspects. Those towns included Newaygo, White Cloud, Grant, Hesperia, Ravenna, and Kent City.

Newaygo had taken last year's league championship, beating most teams by a large margin. However, their squad last year was heavy with seniors, so we figured we had a chance. Only problem was, the heart of our team was now mostly underclassmen as well. Sam Avery and I were sophomores along with Bill Ayers and the other two starters would likely be juniors, Jack Bramer and Louie Hood.

During those early practice sessions, Coach Lewis tossed something new at us. It was a man-to-man full-court press defense, whereas we had always used a shifting zone defense. To our knowledge, no other teams used man-to-man, so we sought to surprise them.

And it did surprise their teams, at least the first two before the word got around from Newaygo and White Cloud. We jumped off to huge leads against both teams, mostly with interceptions as they tried to pass the ball in and under our basket.

We won both games handily by 10 or more points. Then came the remainder of first-round games and the entire season, and the other teams had gotten the word and had practiced against the man-to-man defense.

We lost to Grant and Hesperia by slim margins and then beat Ravenna and Kent City on their courts. It was a long season and I was glad, frankly, when the final game pitted us once more against Grant. It was on our court and it was rough---rough because of what we considered a bunch of tough "onion growers" shoving and pushing us around. The score was tied at the half 39-39, and we went into the second half just feeling lucky enough to be in the game.

Then it happened. I got a pass under the basket from Sam and went up high to lay the ball in. A player on their team, who in later years actually apologized to me for his action, bent down just below me. I went over him and I came down, landing on my head.

I came around several minutes later, lying on the bench. Now in those days not much was known about concussions, but I knew I had a king-sized headache and was groggy.

I remained out of action for the remainder of the game, which we eventually lost in overtime 54-53.

We didn't win the league championship that year and didn't see any district tournament action. Frankly, somehow I was glad it was over...But I did receive my 4th Varsity letter.

Spring brought the track season to us and we fared pretty well. I medaled that year in the 100-yard dash and high jump, and we sent three boys to the State Finals at Lansing. I was not one of them, but I received my 5th Varsity letter for participating in track.

Along with my sophomore year came spring baseball and Coach tried to get me to go out for the team again. As said earlier, father was a huge fan of the Detroit Tigers and had hoped I'd become a baseball player. But ironically, as much as I enjoyed a make-up game or simply pretending to be a major league pitcher while playing catch with Sam, I still wasn't ready to stand in an outfield and watch the grass grow. So the season passed.

Summer was coming on and I was thinking of getting a job. With Dad being an employee of the Conservation Department, it seemed a natural to give them a try, and at that very time they were looking to make up a work crew in our area for stream improvement.

The problem was I wasn't quite 15 and they were hiring boys 17 and older. Now, I'm not certain just how he did it, but I'm certain my Dad pulled a string or two or even won a Friday night poker game, as suddenly I was hired by the State of Michigan.

CHAPTER 13

A Great Summer to Work and "Butterfly Fish"

IN THE STREAM improvement program, crews traveled down big rivers and smaller streams, working on banks that had washed out by rip-rapping with stones and building water-diverter obstructions in the river itself.

Equipment, including a gas-operated air blower, saws, axes, chainsaws and other accessories, was hauled along in a boat as we moved downstream.

It was heavy work but didn't do my muscles any harm. In fact it was toughening me up for fall football. Our work began way upstream on the Middle Branch of the Pere Marquette River below the little town of Chase.

Oh, the town of Chase reminded me that our school's baseball team had a junior pitcher who had a great curveball that no one seemed able to hit. One time, when I grabbed a bat for fun and faced him, he tossed me three strikes that came at me from third base! I'll swear they did. I don't know what ever happened to that young man.

Our stream crew all wore chest-high waders, and we took turns operating the air blower and swinging a hammer to drive in wooden deflector dams. The air blower was used to loosen up the stream bottom as the wooden deflector boards were pounded into the sand.

We carried lunches along with us in the boat and enjoyed lunch times with a lot of horseplay and camaraderie. For me, I reverted to my younger camping-out days and put a line in the water during our lunch time, sometimes catching a dandy trout to take home that late afternoon.

One noon a Conservation Officer walked in to where we were resting and asked who had the "set" line in the water downstream a few hundred feet.

We all looked questioningly at one another and said we were unaware of any lines in the water. The others protected me because they knew it was my fish line.

However, it was a good thing it was my old casting rod, for the officer had grabbed it up and it was gone. Several weeks later, while picking up my check in the Conservation Headquarters building in Baldwin, I saw that same rod hanging on the wall over a desk. Again, I was glad it wasn't my good fly-fishing rod!

I did no more fishing after that while on the stream improvement project.

However, I continued to fish the Pere Marquette River nearly every night. And then one evening I had an extraordinary experience. I called it "butterfly fishing."

Upstream a ways there was a small tributary that went through a round corrugated pipe, and sometimes I was able to land a dandy trout from inside that pipe. On this evening I cradled a half-finished peanut butter and jam sandwich as I leaned over to look in the pipe. Several dandy brown trout lay in there, so I got my fly rod going.

Just then a large and beautiful monarch butterfly flew up in front of me. It actually landed on my shirt near my left elbow. Well, I shook my arm lightly and the butterfly flew off down near the water, then it returned to my elbow once again.

I looked closely then and noticed that it was eating some of the strawberry jam that had accidently rubbed off on my arm from the sandwich. I shook my arm once more and again the butterfly flew out and over the water, only to return quickly to my arm and its jam lunch.

Just then a young boy appeared alongside me and inquired, "Did you ever catch anything in that old pipe?" Now, normally I would let a remark such as that go by, but suddenly my deviltry rose up. I looked closely at the kid.

"Sure," I said. "Watch this." So I shook my arm again and the butterfly fluttered down near the water and again returned to my arm.

"See," I said. "I've got this butterfly trained to spot fish. His name is Pete and he just told me there's a dandy fish in there."

So I let the fly run down inside the pipe, and wham! Shortly I had a nice trout on the bank beside me.

The kid was in total awe. "I don't believe it. Can you do it again?"

"Well, let's just see," I told him. So I shook my arm again and the butterfly flew down and around once more, finally returning to its jam lunch.

"Yep, Ol' Pete just told me there was another one in there." So once more I let the buck-tail fly float into the pipe, and shortly I had another dandy brown trout on the bank beside me.

The young kid was absolutely beside himself by now. He stooped about and remarked, "I believe it because I saw it, and I'm gonna go catch me a butterfly and teach it to spot fish!!!" Then he continued muttering as he disappeared downstream, but I shouted after him, "Give it a try, but I should warn you not to let your butterfly get down too close to the water. A big ol' trout might rise up and grab him, and you wouldn't want your butterfly to get into a jam like that, would you?"

Well, I glanced at my arm and the butterfly was gone, its meal finished. But you can believe that I was all smiles as I wrapped up my fishing for the evening, grabbed up my trout and went home.

CHAPTER 14

Junior Year Football

IN ADDITION TO working hard on stream improvement that summer, and doing a lot of fishing, I worked out with both the football and basketball so I might be prepared for my junior year on the gridiron and on the court.

It was late August when Coach Lewis showed up at my door, looking me over with some approval and remarking, "Well, young man, I see you've grown taller and filled out more. You ready for football?"

I chuckled slightly and replied, "Yes, Coach. I think I'm ready for the game. We have the same schedule this year as last?"

"Exactly the same, but a few of those teams are loaded with juniors and seniors as we are, so it's gonna be a tough season. I'm gonna start backfield practice a little early, ahead of the others, and that's what I want to talk about. Actually, I want to get together with you and a few others beginning next Monday afternoon. I've developed some new plays where we shift from our usual T-formation into a single-wing right or left, with a direct snap from center to the ball carrier. It's a little tricky, but I think we can handle it."

"Some college teams are doing that now," I offered. "Sounds like a winner to me, as we can confuse the other team with the shift and run to where our strength is."

"Exactly," Coach replied as he handed me a small hand-drawn booklet of plays. "Look these over and we'll give 'em a try Monday afternoon after school."

He turned to leave then, but halted to put in a parting word. "In the meantime, not only study the plays but think about who, perhaps, should be in that backfield with you. That's important."

"Okay," I said as he got in his Chevy and exited our driveway.

That weekend I looked carefully at Coach's plays. The sequence was to line up in our old T-formation, then to shout "Shift, one, two, three," and move into our new position. I would take three steps to the right as the right halfback took two steps and lined up right behind me. The left halfback would be in position to receive a direct snap from center. In such a scheme, any one of the four in the backfield was actually in a position to receive a direct snap from center.

Then one thing dawned on me and Sunday afternoon I called Coach. "Coach, we'll need Willie Monday at center, so we can get in some snaps."

"Right," he answered. "I'll call him and make sure he's there. And who do you suggest for the backfield?"

"Well, Whitey at right half, Hood at fullback, and Bitely at left half will be good for starters," I told him, "assuming they're all coming out."

"They'll all come out or I'll have their tails!" Coach remarked with a laugh. "See you there."

Monday afternoon after school, we met over at our "turkey-patch" football field to go over Coach's new plays. His plays really weren't difficult, but they depended on positioning and timing.

We started with "Wing right 2", where I get the snap from Willie after the shift and "Set, signals, hut-1" and gave an inside handoff to Whitey who was charging through the 2-hole, just right of center. We ran that play about a dozen times before trying the opposite play, "Wing left 2." Both were pretty simple and both gave the opposite halfback time to charge through the same hole ahead of the ball carrier and run interference or block. The one obvious play was "Fullback Spinner" where Hood took Willie's direct snap, faked as he spun around to the halfback and then ran to daylight through the line.

There were other similar plays and three new passing plays, where I got a direct snap from Willie and dropped back, with all three backs blocking in front of me. From that position the fullback could sort of drift off to the left or right to receive a pass. That play, through the coming season, would become one of my favorites.

In three weeks we would play Newaygo at home, so most of our practices were geared toward the line and its blocking assignments.

So we had some new plays and most of the linemen found their new assignments and reacted well.

That still left our defense to deal with, and for the first time I found I wasn't assigned to the safety position but on the sidelines assigned to Coach, where we could have time to discuss the next series of offensive plays. I liked that idea, and not just because I had time to gather plays and assignments, but because during the preceding season I'd been getting killed out there!

CHAPTER 15

Good times on the Gridiron

ALTHOUGH OUR FOOTBALL team had had limited success during my freshman year, it had not been a good year when I was a sophomore. I hadn't been able to play due to that two-month long heart murmur the Doc said I had, and it had been a long fall season for me.

Now I felt good and ready to go. Practices went well and spirits were high on the entire team.

Two weeks after school started, we were ready for our first game. Newaygo would visit us at our "turkey patch," and we wanted to pay back last year's loss.

We did. Hood took the opening kick at the 30-yard line and raced down the left sideline to the end zone. Judd Copeland booted the extra point and we had a 7-zip opening lead. Our defense held on the next series and they punted to our 40-yard line.

It was our first opportunity to use our single-wing offense, and our shift from the T into it confused their defense. I took the snap from Willie and stepped back to pass. Hood, as we'd practiced, drifted off to the left a few yards and headed down the field, wide open. I hit him with a bullet and off he went, untouched for his second touchdown.

Newaygo's coach was furious. He called time and lectured his defense loudly on their sidelines. "Okay, girls, it's time to get serious! We're better than this, so get our game moving and remember your assignments!"

I was certain the small crowd and students heard him, because both benches and all the seating were on the west sidelines. It was like a little Hollywood Bowl, without the Hollywood part!

Oh, but I was in Seventh Heaven. This was my first football game since my freshman year, we were already winning, and I was feeling great...for the time being, anyway.

It was Newaygo's turn, and they moved the kick-off ball from their 35-yard line right down to our 15-yard line. On the next first-down play, their quarterback threw a quick look-'n-pass to their left end, and they scored. Their kicker missed the extra point and the score was 14-6.

We failed to get a first down on the next series, and I dropped back to punt the ball. I'd usually get a decent punt off, but this time I caught it just right and got off a long spiral that went out of bounds just inside their 5-yard-line. I glanced at the sidelines and Coach Lewis stood there grinning ear-to-ear.

From that moment on the game was ours. We got our third touchdown on a 22-right-run by Whitey in the third quarter, and we won the game 21-6.

Our second game was at White Cloud and they must have scouted our game with Newaygo because they were ready for our shift and single-wing offense. We made little progress on our first two plays on offense, so I called a play we pulled out of a college game. It was "student body right," and when the ball was hiked, the entire line and backfield ran right, supposedly to run interference and block for me after I received the snap in the T-formation.

The ball snapped into my hands and I took one step back to swivel and follow the crowd. But Willie pulled out from center and all 220 pounds of him crushed my right foot.

I ran out the play, which went for a nearly impossible 18-yards, and came back to the huddle limping. I knew something was wrong around the area of my toes, but it wasn't going to stop me. Not today!

I played on offense the rest of the game and tried to avoid the pain. We scored twice in the second half and won the game 14-0.

When we got on the bus to go home, I took my right shoe off and observed the damage. The big toe had been snapped out of joint and was actually leaning on the second toe. But there was no blood and actually little pain.

Coach Lewis was right there by me and told me to get to the doctor's office first thing in the morning.

That was Saturday morning, and Dr. M. took one look and said, "You were lucky at that. Nothing's broken and it may be best to simply leave it as it is. If I try to snap the toe back straight, it may break, and if that happens, you're done with football for the season."

I nearly exploded off the bench I was sitting on and shot back, "Let's leave it alone; I can handle it!"

We went through our remaining games with fairly good results. We topped Grant 21-13 and Hesperia, ironically, by an identical score.

Ravenna was having one of its better seasons and a missed extra point turned into a loss, 14-13.

Our final game that season was at Kent City and we ran over the "onion-growers" by a score of 34-14.

After that game and on the bus going home, Coach Lewis stood up and spoke to us. "Boys, we've just completed a remarkable season. Only one loss! Actually, a season like this would qualify us for state-wide play-offs in Class D, if we had such play-offs. Many coaches throughout the state have been lobbying for those, and it just could come true for next year. That's no relief for you seniors who will be graduating this school year, but you juniors and below may have a shot at it. Let's hope so!"

Everyone on the bus broke into a cheer and Coach smiled broadly as he took his seat.

I sort of dozed off during the ride back to Baldwin, but I guess I was pleased inside. I'd just earned my 6th Varsity letter…But who was counting?

CHAPTER 16

A Deer Hunt and a
Great Basketball Season

THERE WASN'T MUCH time to waste between the football and basketball seasons. It seems we stepped right off the gridiron onto the court, with only a few weeks until 12 games of basketball became imminent.

But there was one interruption and that was bow and arrow deer season. Coach once again asked if I wanted to join him to hunt near his brother's place on Hess Lake near Newaygo.

So off we went on November 15, early in the morning. I hadn't had much practice with the bow that year and the first thing I saw after we were in the woods was a dandy spike-horn buck coming right at me.

He moved slowly, but he wasn't downwind of me, so I don't think he knew I was in the same woods. Then he suddenly stopped and turned broadside of me, only about 20 yards away.

As I said, a lack of practice along with some buck fever added up as I drew the bow string and released it, watching the arrow glance right off the deer's back!

But the deer made a fatal mistake. It ran straight in the direction of Coach and his shot didn't miss.

So that was it. After field-dressing it, we hauled the deer to his brother's garage where we hung it up. His brother said he'd cut it up and package it for Coach. With that, my deer season was over, except that one evening Coach showed up at our house and handed my Mom several packages of venison. She loved venison, was a good cook, and was all smiles.

The other thing I have to say about my missing a hit on that deer was that many times I'd get up on the roof of the garage and shoot at a downward angle at a paper plate attached to a bale of hay. I could hit that target about every time, but the problem was that I never saw a deer in the woods with a paper plate attached to its side! Makes sense, right?

Basketball practice was going full tilt and Coach had lined up a non-conference game over at Custer, a small town west of Baldwin.

They had a "cracker-box-size" gym that I took advantage of to rack up 37 points, the most I ever scored in any game.

Coach took us aside at the next practice and threw a curve at us. "Boys," he said, "starting this season there's going to be state-wide play-offs in basketball. That means that if we win half of our six games, we'll be eligible for the play-offs. Do you think we can do it?"

Well, a gigantic "Yes!" went up from the entire team and we seemed to be bouncing on air all over the gym that afternoon. We had a good team and we knew it!

Newaygo had a good team too. They were leading us 32-25 at the half and I was trying to score but the basket seemed to have a lid on it.

During the half, Coach took me aside and offered some good advice. "Ed, Bill is taller than the guys guarding him, so pass the ball in high to him and see what happens."

I did, and Bill our center scored 22 points in the second half! We won 67-52 and we couldn't have done it without him.

After that win, Coach asked me if I learned anything. He asked it in an easy voice and wasn't angry about it. Rather, from the locker bench I looked up at him and replied, "Pass the ball, right?"

"Right," he said with a grin. Then he passed the ball, which got me good in the belly, and walked away.

He was certainly correct. The rest of the league was obviously told to key in on me and this gave my teammates opportunities to be open and score. They did, and it made me pleased. No one that I know of had actually called me a "ball-hog," but I felt as though I'd been one. And now, passing the basketball seemed as good as scoring.

We were in a scoring bonanza and won our next three games against White Cloud, Grant and Hesperia.

Then came Ravenna and we played our first overtime game. I don't know where they got 'em, but they had three starters this season that were well over 6-feet tall. Actually, we were tied 37-37 at the half and at the final buzzer it was 66-66.

We traded buckets in overtime, and Jack Bramer threw up a desperation shot almost from half-court at the buzzer. The ball bounced straight up off the rim and down through the hoop! We carried Jack off the court on our shoulders following that single-point victory.

We won our remaining game against Kent City and all of them during a return engagement with each of the six teams. With those wins we had captured the 1951 NCAA Championship and were looking forward to the Final Championship games. They were District, Regional and State Finals down in Lansing.

Ah, but I suppose we were a bit ahead of ourselves. By a year, I'd say. We ran up against a team from Leroy in the District finals and they whipped us by 11 points!

It was a sour ending to a great year on the court, but at a team banquet held in our honor, Coach Lewis talked to all of us, players and parents alike.

"We have just been through an amazing basketball year for Baldwin High School," he said. "These boys won 11 of 12 games, something no other team in our league to my knowledge has accomplished in the past.

"Yes, we lost in the play-offs, but let's not dwell on that. I'll take the blame for the loss. I didn't have our team prepared for that game.

"So let's look to the future. We'll lose our seniors for next year, but thank God we had them this year. They performed well and helped us win those 11 games. However, we have many boys returning next year for their senior year and I can see, prophetically, not only a League Championship, but a District, Regional and likely a State Championship!"

The place went wild as he sat down! We loved Coach Lewis.

CHAPTER 17

Track and Baseball

THE WINTER CAME and went, and as spring became imminent my thoughts turned to track, where as a Junior I would be trying to excel in the 100-yard dash, the long jump and the high jump.

Ah, but spring baseball was also coming and our man "for all the seasons", Coach Lewis, approached me in the hallway one afternoon in April.

"Well," he said, "he's done it again. Bob, our second baseman, got angry at me and quit the team, just as he did back in football several years ago."

He paused and I just knew what was coming. "Eddie, how'd you like to try your hand at second base? I've seen you play some and you could handle it. You'll be involved in spring sports, track and baseball, but I think we can work 'em both in. What do ya' say?"

"Well, Coach," I replied with a grin. "I never thought of becoming another Jessie Owens at track, so I'll give baseball a try if you believe I can help."

We held some of our baseball practices inside in the same gym where we played basketball, and much of it was simply playing catch and conditioning. There was only some hitting in a cage, where the baseball wouldn't crash the windows and make the place look like a war zone any more than it already was.

It got more realistic when we finally were able to get out to our baseball field. There we had fielding practice, pitching, and lots of hitting.

Our first game came up quick, and we were rained out. I figured no game to be a blessing, as it was also colder outside than a well-diggin' auger.

But Coach, with his usual ingenuity, lined up a game over at Scottville, about 20 miles west of Baldwin. It would fill in for what would have been a game down at White Cloud.

I was no pro at second base, but found I was hitting very well and on my third trip to the plate, with two guys on base, one on second base and one on first, I somehow connected on a curve ball that sailed high and over the outfield fence. That hit was one of only three I got during our first two games, and I still have that ball… somewhere!

Well, I was having fun running from the baseball field to the track area, when it came to a halt with startling swiftness. Coach called me over after our second game and sort of looked at me as though he was about to pull a rug out from under my feet.

"Ed," he said with a serious look, "Bob wants back on the team. He's apologized and promises to play good ball. I could let him take second base again and you could concentrate on track." He paused, and then said, "But it's strictly up to you. What do you say?"

Actually, although I didn't want to show it, I was somewhat relieved. "Coach," I got out, "that's fine with me. Baseball isn't really my game anyway."

So that ended my baseball career then and there. But I smiled to myself as I walked away. After all, having played in a couple of games, I'd also earned my 8th Varsity letter.

So now I could concentrate on track, which would wrap up my junior year at Baldwin along with a 9th Varsity letter.

I was amazed at this year's situation on the track field. For openers, I no longer had the best times in the 100-yard dash. A black boy named Ernie bested me by a full second. I was still best in the long jump by more than a foot, but came in a close third in the high jump.

Coach wanted me to try something new, so he told me to try the pole vault. Now, in those days we didn't have anything but sand in the landing pit, and the poles were aluminum with little bending action like the new ones do as you take to the air.

We did have a wooden insert where you placed the pole as you went up, and on my second attempt, at about a near 7-feet, I missed that insert and went flat on my back on the wood. My days of pole vaulting ended right there.

We really didn't have a complete quarter-mile track at our field, so any distance running or passing of the baton was simply practiced on a straight run, and that was at the football field.

We had only two track meets that spring, one at White Cloud and one at Newaygo. Usually, all seven schools participated, but sometimes several schools didn't show up for one reason or another.

In the meet at White Cloud with only four schools participating, our school's chance of winning it was very good. And we did win. We took 1-2 in the 100, 1-2 in the high jump 1-3 in the broad jump, and won the 880 relay by several yards. It was a fun event.

Newaygo was not so easy. I stumbled when the starter's gun went off for the 100 dash and didn't even finish it. None of my teammates nor I could get any height in the high jump, and we came in 3-4 in the broad jump as well.

So Newaygo was not a good meet, but our win back in White Cloud meet did qualify several of us to attend the Michigan State Finals in Lansing.

There were only four of us going to the Finals, so Coach drove us down in his car, a new Chevrolet he'd purchased from Cronk's Chevy Sales in Baldwin.

It was a fun trip, but we didn't win much. Class D was loaded with talent that year, so four of us medaled in the 880 relay and I came in a distant fourth in the broad jump.

Several of us got Varsity letters for track as juniors that year. It was my 9th, but to be honest I'd almost quit counting.

Summer was coming, I was turning 17 and I would be looking for a summer job.

CHAPTER 18

A U.S. Forestry Hero

BALDWIN HAD A U.S. Forestry Service headquarters that looked after several thousand acres of forests, including the Huron/Manistee National Forest.

Sam Avery, a buddy I've mentioned before, got wind that they'd be hiring about 10 young guys to fight fires and work in the tree plantations that summer, so we went together to apply. We were hired on the spot.

All of us were to arrive at headquarters by 7:30 a.m. each week day, and each morning the first thing we'd do is raise Old Glory over the Ranger Station. I guess that's where I learned to respect the American flag.

We were all there and on duty on the Fourth of July, and it was a summer with a temperature in the 90s and forest fire danger rampant throughout the dry woods.

So fighting fires was our primary duty. But there was a secondary job equally as tiring. On this day we were to continue that job – working in the young pine plantations. Each of us was given an axe and were encouraged to keep it razor sharp. All ten of us would grab our axes and stretch out in a straight line. Then we walked through the plantations "girdling" (cutting out a ring of bark) the larger trees so they would eventually die, leaving the young pines to grow faster and straighter.

Joe Mack, many years a forester, was our crew chief and in charge while working the plantation or fighting fires. He was heavy-set and muscular man with intense eyes. He was also an avid hunter and fisherman and had a habit of joking or pulling pranks on us boys.

But on one particular day he wasn't kidding when he came charging through the brush yelling, "Fire! Fire!"

We had no such thing as a drill, so we knew this was the real thing. And this was the Fourth of July. We flung our axes and ourselves into the truck and went bouncing off through the woods with Joe at the wheel.

About then most of us were getting pretty scared. On a hot and windy day we figured the fire would be a bad one. It was, and we could smell and see the smoke when several miles away.

The fire had started about five miles west of Wolf Lake in Lake County and had already burned off several square miles.

We unloaded about a mile east of what would become our fire line. Then we exchanged our axes for "Indian pumpers", called that because you strapped them on your back like a papoose. They weighed about 80 pounds when full of water and had a pumping hose and nozzle you worked by hand.

Our crew strung out in that same straight line we used when girdling trees and headed toward the fire.

Then there it was, snapping and crackling its way toward us at an alarming pace. Sped on by the wind, we could see it flashing in "top fires" up high in some of the trees while we could see some of the older trees literally falling over in the wind and fire.

Shortly, we reached a point where the forestry plow had gone through in an attempt to make a wide, deep ditch, intending to help arrest the fire. This rut became our fire line and our job was to try to stop the fire from jumping that ditch.

As the flames and smoke intensified, it became next to impossible to either see or hear anyone around you, although we were supposed to be about 12 paces from one another. Then, we could no longer keep the flames from going beyond us, while the wind and top fires spread, so that we were nearly surrounded by flames. Suddenly Joe's booming voice came through the din, "Fall back! Fall back!"

It was just at that moment, as I recall, there was a loud, cracking sound, and I looked up to see an old oak tree coming down right at me. Its main trunk was off to my right while its upper branches were wide spread and on fire. I wasn't able to jump fast and far enough to totally escape so some branches knocked me flat. I wasn't knocked out, just stunned, but probably could have "bought the farm", as the saying goes.

Suddenly, Joe's eagle-like face was peering down at me. He'd retreated with the rest, but saw I was missing and returned for me. He then helped me out of the pumper straps and flung the thing aside. Then he lifted me up and the two of us, nearly overcome by the stifling smoke, wove a scrambled path back to the truck and safety.

We were to fight that fire three more sweltering days and many others that summer.

Some years ago Joe went on to the "Happy Hunting Grounds." He had 30 years in the U.S. Forest Service and lived in Hesperia, Michigan.

But that Fourth of July is one I shall never forget. And, although I've had several "heroes" during my lifetime, Joe Mack is right at the top of that list....and he will always be there.

So my summer with the U.S. Forest Service came to an end, but long before it did I'd been thinking of the coming football season and my senior year.

CHAPTER 19

Senior Football Begins

THAT SUMMER OF swinging an axe and fighting fires seemed to build my strength and durability, and now I was ready for my senior year at Baldwin High School.

Coach had me along with the entire backfield and ends practicing about two weeks before school actually started. I had to end my forestry job early in order to participate three nights each week.

We kept the practice section rather secretive and didn't practice at our football field but at a large, vacant lot near my home.

Coach Lewis went over a prospective "starter" list with me, and it was getting tough to say who would be in what position. Mostly, it would be seniors sprinkled with a couple of juniors and one sophomore too.

Whitey had graduated, so right halfback needed to be filled, along with Jack's end position. But we still had Hood for that right-half spot along with Ayers at the left end. Willie Horner, the one who'd ruined my right toe, would be at left halfback, and Center would fall either to Lee, my backup, or to Jack Bramer. Fullback was undecided, and the guards and tacklers would be determined as we practiced.

We finally gave Clarence Bitely a try at fullback. He was strong and very athletic, but his only problem was remembering where to go on each play. That could be a real problem so we kept trying guys.

After the second evening of practice, Coach once again showed up at my house. He had several papers in hand and wanted my attention for a few minutes.

He had sketched out several new pass plays that went beyond the range of our 10-left and 10-right plays that were square outs. These went deep into the secondary, and blocking was critical on the line and backs as well.

Coach told me a major difference in long-pass plays was it takes the quarterback longer to get the pass off, up to four or five seconds or even longer, and one can't pass if he's flat on his back or running for his life.

So enter the prospective linemen—two guards and two tacklers. Their job as with the center was critical to the success of the play. Judd Copeland and Ivan Ives worked out the best physically, and also were smart enough to remember to perform their assignments. We installed them at the left and right-guard positions. We kept trying for guys who'd fit the bill at tackles, and found no one that really was smart or physical enough to do the job. We set it aside for the moment.

When regular practice began, coinciding with the first day of school, we started concentrating on defense and conditioning. I found that I was back at safety on defense, but felt a lot of the exercises and running weren't really necessary. After all, I'd just spent the entire summer swinging an axe and making end-runs around or through fires!

Our six-game schedule loomed up almost overnight and it was the usual suspects we'd be up against. Again, there would be our usual opener against Newaygo, followed by White Cloud, Grant and Hesperia, with away games against Ravenna and Kent City.

The second game, White Cloud at home, would be our Homecoming game. I was looking forward to it, not only for the football, but I'd already been voted Homecoming King. And to top it off, Carol, a junior, would be Homecoming Queen, and I really liked her.

Until this point I'd had little to do with girls. There was one I dated a few times, Janet, but she was only a sophomore, although in stature she walked and acted much older. Even though she was only 15, she could likely have passed for a college student!

The day prior to our first game I really had the jitters. I rationalized it may be because trout season was closing for the fall and winter and I'd grossly neglected fishing that summer. No, it couldn't be that! Perhaps it was because I'd recently purchased an old 1939 Mercury with Forest Service pay and hadn't had much chance to use it. Then I cleared my head and realized that this would be my last span of time at Baldwin to play football, basketball and run track. That had to be it, and if so then I had to do my best.

So that Friday night we traveled down to Newaygo's field. We kicked off, having lost the coin toss, and our defense held them to a six-yard gain. They punted and I received the ball around the 40-yard line. Our entire team took off, blocking as I ran, and I ran out of bounds around their 40-yard line. Two guys hit me at once and I suddenly knew this was not going to be a fun game.

Earlier I'd asked Coach if I could take the opening kickoff, and he'd agreed with some reservation and a remark that I was needed as quarterback. Well, he was right in several ways and I decided to have Hood or Bramer take the kick-offs henceforth!

Our opening play was a fake hand-off to Hood and a post-pattern pass to Ayers. It worked, as Hood was tackled by about five guys going through the line and I turned to see Ayers wide open. I threw the pass, leading him by a good margin, and he almost walked into the end zone with our first touchdown.

Copeland kicked off and the receiver ran the ball back to mid-field. It appeared that Newaygo had improved since last season, as they moved the ball on the ground to the one-yard line, where their quarterback dove over center to score. Just like that, it became a tied game.

Newaygo's linemen matched up well with ours, both offensively and defensively, and the first quarter ended with both teams punting several times. Actually, all the linemen on both sides appeared gassed, hands on hips and huffing and puffing like the big bad wolf.

And one of their "wolves" took the second quarter kick-off and went straight up the center of the field to score. It was a rapid quarter with few mistakes on either side. At least that was defensively. It was like "our front-line five can beat your front-line five."

So we punted back and forth to end the first half, 14-7 in their favor.

Their players were obviously overjoyed and jumped about, celebrating as they left the field. Rather than get back on the bus for half-time, Coach said we'd all sit down under a goal post at one end of the field and talk awhile as we watched the grass grow. We all laughed and then sat and listened.

CHAPTER 20

The Coach talked and
we paid attention!

"MEN," COACH BEGAN as he looked over our team seated on the ground, "we're at half-time in our first game of the season and we're behind. But we're not going to be on the short end when this game is over."

He paused as though to let that sink in, then said, "We've been through four weeks of practice up to this game and I've seen some improvement in the first half of this game, particularly on defense. I know we can do it because we've paid particular attention to conditioning. And in the second half, especially in the fourth quarter, the team that remains the strongest, not walking around with their hands on their hips, will usually be the winner. Tonight that's going to be us." He paused once more and said, "You interior line men," he looked at those individuals for a long moment, "guards and tackles, you have it in your hands to win this game. And I'm not simply talking about one or the other, offense or defense, but both."

He walked about as he continued, "We're not just going to win this first game, but every one of them, and we have six and a half to play."

After another long pause he said, "We are a small Class D School. All of the teams we play are from larger schools. In fact, our graduating senior class, including girls, will only be about 30-35 students this coming spring. Only five of our entire team are seniors. The rest of you are underclassmen.

"Now, we'll be kicking off to begin the third quarter and I want you to stop them on every play. Some of you are going both ways, offense and defense, but remain strong and show them what we've got. Let's go!"

"Go Blue! Go Gold!" was the battle cry as we ran to our sideline, did a few exercises, and took to the field for the second half.

Copeland kicked off for us and he got off a beauty. It sailed clean over the receiver's head and rolled to their three-yard line where two of them jumped on it.

Our defense went to work then. Newaygo gained just seven yards and their kicker set up in the end zone to punt the ball.

Their center hiked the ball and their punter took two steps forward to kick it. That was disastrous for them, as Ivan broke through their line and knocked the ball down into their end zone where Kinney jumped on it for a touchdown. Following the extra-point kick by Copeland, we were in a tie game, 14-14.

It was a demoralizing turn of events for Newaygo and they failed to score for the remainder of the game. Our defense held them to less than 40 yards during the second half, while our offense scored on two pass plays to gain the final 28-14 victory for Baldwin.

The bus ride home from that first game was exciting, but now we had White Cloud to look forward to the next Friday, and that would be Homecoming.

CHAPTER 21

"Homecoming"

THE BAND WAS playing, floats surrounded the field, people were cheering, and there was, as I recall, bedlam everywhere. There was almost enough noise to upset the referee at the coin toss!

The ref tossed a fifty-cent piece in the air and it landed standing straight up on edge in the sand! Rather befuddled, he muttered something that sounded like, "Hey, that never happened before." Then he gathered himself and flipped the coin again.

We lost and White Cloud wanted the ball first.

Now, I don't know where White Cloud got such a "gorilla", but their big guy gobbled up Copeland's kick at their 11-yard line, went straight up the middle of the field as he dispatched our defenders one after another with straight arms. In no time he stood all alone in our end zone with a huge grin on his face!

Our crowd went silent and was wondering what happened as their quarterback passed to his left-end for a 2-point conversion and the score was suddenly 8-0.

The game was scarcely a minute old as they kicked off to us. Elmer Hood gathered in the bouncing football at our 25-yard line and headed for some open ground near the left sideline. He was met there by several defensive players and shoved out of bounds around the 30-yard line.

Five of our guys played both offense and defense, so six exchanged places and our offense was on the field. I called a simple line play and then let up under Willie at center. I was supposed to hand the ball off to our right halfback, but just before Willie snapped the ball to me, I glanced to my left and Bill Ayers stood out there all by himself. Nobody was even near him and he was looking back to me. They had blown the coverage.

I was so excited to get the play off that I nearly dropped the ball when Willie hiked it. I pivoted to my right and watched the surprised look on our fullback's face when I didn't hand it off to him, but took several steps back, spun around and looked to see Bill as he took a couple of steps up the field and turned left toward the sideline. There was no player within 15 yards of him as he headed up the field and I passed the ball, leading him by several feet.

Bill gathered in the football and raced untouched up the sideline to the end zone. We had our touchdown, but I opted to kick the extra point rather than go for a 2-point conversion. Willie hiked the ball back to me and I put it down on its nose as Judd Copeland stepped up and hit it. The ball went up and careened backward off the goal post crossbar.

So we stood at 8-6 in White Cloud's favor at half-time.

For me, this half-time was like recess at school and I was Homecoming King. Carol, Homecoming Queen, stood with me in front of the band as we were introduced. She turned, looked at me, and planted a kiss on my cheek. I about fainted. Soon it was over, however, as her court was introduced and it was announced that the Junior float won the yearly float contest.

White Cloud kicked to us to begin the second half. Ivan Ives, who normally played right tackle on offense, was in a position to receive the kick-off, and he grabbed it just as though he knew where he was going.

Ivan was not a big kid, only about 150 pounds, but he was very strong, wiry and fast. Actually, he was somewhat undersized for a position at tackle, but he made up for that with his quickness and strength. He quickly wove his way through the defense and wasn't stopped until he reached their 47-yard line. I was near him and helped him to his feet. He gave me a look that was actually funny, with dirt on his face and a toothy grin. "Thanks, I needed that!" was all he said.

The remainder of most of the second half was give and take, more like a tug of war with the defenses on both sides. Then, with about six minutes remaining, I thought of that old 10-right end play we'd used over and over in a game a season or two before, and called it in a "hurry-up" huddle. Jack, at right end, was to take two strides forward and cut to the right sideline into the flat.

The play worked, giving us about 10 yards, so I called it again. Fact is, I called that play six times in a row, and suddenly we were at their 9-yard line, with Jack looking at me as though he may kill me if I called it again. But I did call it again, and we lined up. However, this time I handed off to Whitey rather than fake it to him, and he went straight between Willie and Ivan, untouched and into the end zone. Judd kicked the extra point and we led White Cloud, 13-8.

We kicked off with only four minutes remaining in the game. I was behind our defense and watched as their "gorilla" gobbled up the ball around his own 40-yard line and headed straight down the middle of the field. Our defense seemed to be wiped to the ground as the big guy knocked players aside like ten-pins. Then he was headed straight at me, and I could see a big grin on his face as he anticipated wiping this "mosquito" away as well!

The huge player was right in front of me when I fell to the ground backward and whipped out my right arm. I caught his right foot around the ankle and he nearly pulled my arm out of its socket as he fell forward, flat on his face. The wind was knocked out of the guy and he was helped off the field by some teammates. Déjà vu!

At that junction there was less than two minutes to play, and time expired following two short-yardage plays.

The Homecoming Game was over, 13-8. Our second game of the season was completed and we were joyfully surrounded by happy parents, classmates and faculty.

CHAPTER 22

Completing the Season

IN **THE EARLY** years we had no "play-offs" to determine District, Regional and State Football Championship teams. You settled with what you were able to accomplish within your own League. Our League actually had two titles – we won the NCAA (North Central Athletic Association), and also the Newaygo County Athletic Association, depending upon which you preferred, although we were in Lake County.

This resulted in the fact that when our regular football games were played, our season was ended. So we still had several games to play and it was a matter of pleasing our Coach, our fans, our school and ourselves. There would be no medals for 1st, 2nd or 3rd place as was the case with basketball and track.

So we still had four football games scheduled. They were with Grant, Hesperia, Ravenna and Kent city.

Such games would be wrapping up my high school football career, but I thought I may still have a chance in college, provided I was able to attend one.

I really had no idea at the time what an honor it was to quarterback a football team. I was simply in my third year at the helm of Baldwin's team, and I was having the time of my life.

When football season came around each year, I nearly forgot about fishing or hunting, or anything else but those games. This year was no different as I concentrated on these individual games.

Coach Lewis and I talked frequently and seriously before each of the next four games.

I'm not certain where Coach Lewis got his information concerning the strategies and plays of opposing teams, because we had no "spies" out there to watch other teams – not in those years – but he would tell me which plays would likely work best in certain situations. On defense he would alternate a play with his calls, so the situations were pretty well covered.

During this senior year the Coach let me call nearly all offensive plays, and this gave me a lot of respect among my comrades.

Our third game was at Grant. We called them "the Grant Onion Growers" as Grant called itself "the Onion Capitol of Michigan." And they had some big farm boys to prove it. Our line wasn't a good match for their defense and I spent more time on my back than I did standing up.

The score stood at 0-0 at the beginning of the fourth quarter and near the end of the game, I had a bit of luck. I punted on fourth down from around our 20-yard line, and got off a high spiral that went way over their players' heads, rolling to a stop at Grant's 4-yard line. But what was amazing was that no Grant player went after the ball, and Louie Hood jumped on it.

With less than a minute to play, I called a quarterback sneak, and dove between Willie and Ivan for a touchdown. So we won the game 6-0 and didn't bother to line up for the extra point.

Our fourth game saw Hesperia visiting our field and it wasn't much of a contest. We scored on our first two possessions in the first quarter and went on to win the game 27-12. Coach mentioned following the game that their coach said he had four players out with some sort of bug, and those players were key to his game. So we didn't feel so great and wonderful after all on that bus ride home.

Our fifth game was with the Ravenna Bulldogs, at their field, and again we had a fight on our hands. They held on nearly every defensive play, while they opened huge holes on offense for their runners.

It was one of those games where things just seemed to fall apart. I had two passes intercepted and a blocked punt, as we struggled through the first half, while they scored twice to make it 14-0 at half-time.

In the fourth quarter with about three minutes remaining, I stepped back to pass and two of their players came in from the side and met me at the middle. I hit the ground and the lights went out. I awoke lying on the bench as time expired in the game and upon coming around found that their first-half score had held up. We lost 14-0 to Ravenna.

The following Friday found Kent City coming to our field. It would be my final football game for Baldwin High School and I intended to make the most of it.

Kent City is located near Grand Rapids, and although a small school, they seemed to have a lot of talent to draw from and in their line-ups. They had a quarterback

ED GILBERT

that was well over 6-feet tall, a good passer, and saw the field well.

They won the coin toss and their first play from scrimmage was from their own 35-yard line. Their quarterback fired three straight passes into the flats to give them a first down just over the 50-yard stripe.

I was in my usual defensive position at safety for this game and was figuring that they'd now likely pass over the middle when they did just that. I jumped the play when I saw their right end come across and slant toward the middle, right toward me.

The pass was on its way and their player stretched out his arm to gather it in. I was a step too late, and the football went straight into his arms. But a weird thing happened. The ball slipped right through his hands and hit me square on my number 22.

I had the ball and headed for the left sideline, thinking at least I'd get a few yards before getting smeared. But suddenly, the players nearby who were escorting me down the field were my own guys! I was accompanied by three defensemen and they took me right down the field and into the end zone!

The score was 6-0 and the extra point kick was missed. But that turned out to be the only score of the first half.

Coach Lewis gathered us under a goal post at half-time and opened up with a different look at this game.

"We're having a good game," he said, looking around at our 21 players as he pivoted about the circle, "and I want all of you to know how proud I am of this season. You're going to win this game, and for you seniors it's your last one. So make it your best.

"But, you know, I'm really proud of you guys. So proud, in fact, that I really don't care about the score at the end of this one – win or lose. I'd take you guys into a state play-off if we had one. Someday we'll have one for a team like this!

"Now, go get in a few warm-ups before the second half and play your best for the old Blue and Gold."

A cheer went up and we jumped up to get ready for the second half, my last in the game of football.

And that 6-0 score held up during the second half, as we clocked out our final game of 1951 season in our favor.

In the shower room that evening, I thought, "Well, this is it – my 10th Varsity letter. But, the real letter had been only the first one three years ago; now I have 9 pieces of paper."

Then I said to myself, sarcastically, "What a wonderful thing, eh?"

CHAPTER 23

The 1951-52 League Championship

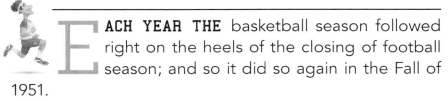**ACH YEAR THE** basketball season followed right on the heels of the closing of football season; and so it did so again in the Fall of 1951.

We hardly had time to turn in our football jerseys, pads and helmets, and put our cleats away before Coach was prodding us into hitting the gymnasium – the same every year.

Well now, Coach knew what I knew: We had all of our starting five returning this year and much would be expected of us. We would, of course, win the District Championship of 1951, would take the Regional easily and wind up in the State play-offs…Fine, but not as easy as it would seem. But first things first. We needed to play all the usual suspects twice from our own district, once on their court and once on ours.

Again, we would be traveling to Newaygo for our first game, and that would be only two weeks from playing on the gridiron. So we ran through our usual skills, the floor work, passing, shooting and some plays.

But Coach pulled something new on us this year. Rather than the other years of 1½ hour practices, we would stretch that time to 2½ hours.

The day he instigated that change he called a meeting and explained. "We're going to a longer practice time for good reason. I want us in such good condition so that we can sustain our speed and strength. By the beginning of the third quarter, when the other team is leaning over and grabbing their socks for lack of breath, we're going to keep going at full speed – just like in football."

Well, the extra practice time was fine with most of us, but a couple of good prospects were juniors and had after-school jobs to contend with. They complained a little, but evidently settled it with their employers and stuck with the extra practice time.

So the first two months of school had come and gone. November was in the wings, with basketball season on deck.

We had the same lineup again – we'd play Newaygo, White Cloud, Grant, Hesperia and Ravenna. Only Kent City would be out this season as they were in another league. We'd play a total of 10 games rather than 12.

But first, Coach had another surprise for us. "We're going to play a couple of practice games," he announced. "We're going to go over and play Luther and then up to Custer for a game. They're both small schools, even smaller than we are in Class D, but it will be good experience for us and for them as well."

So that Tuesday evening we took a bus over to the little hamlet of Luther. They had a small gym, and you couldn't put any arch on the ball as it would bounce off the ceiling. We scored fast and often and it wasn't much of a contest, but good practice. As I recall, we tripled the score on them.

Two evenings later, rather than practice, we took the bus again, this time to Custer. Again, it was a small school with not many good players to choose from.

Now I was a guard, not a forward, but somehow I found myself very often down in the right forward position, where I pumped in 32 points. Actually, I'd been trying to perfect my right hook shot, and that evening it came together. I had few set shots too, mostly hooks, and they went in unconsciously. That shot would serve me well in some games to follow.

So our first league games were with Newaygo and White Cloud and Sam Avery and I had no problem feeding the ball into Bill Ayers at center, where he was quick and accurate to the basket. We won over Newaygo by 17 points and over White Cloud by 23. I scored 19 and Ayers, 22.

The Coach mentioned one day that that our team was getting noticed. The local paper, the Lake County Star, was giving us a good write-up and we were now being mentioned in the Grand Rapids Press in their Saturday or Sunday papers. It was nothing exciting, mind you, just the news and a few players mentioned. These were Ayers and I, and we sort of played it down.

Our following two games were with Grant and Hesperia. We took both in stride, winning each by a margin of 15 and 11, respectively.

The final games of the regular season were with Hesperia and Ravenna, playing all on Friday nights before packed crowds. Our team was clicking on all cylinders and we were in those finals going away.

Actually, I believe we were getting a little carried away with our success as we looked forward to the

District and Regional contests. It almost seemed as though we were funning with the game of basketball.

But Coach Lewis would have none of it. Following our final regular season game with Ravenna, he made us gather in the bleachers and gave us the following talk:

"Look, hot-shots," he began, pausing to glance around and look each of us in the eyes, "I'm not pleased with your attitude of late. Yes, we just completed an undefeated season, our first and the only one in Baldwin High's history. But that doesn't call for believing we're better than sliced bread....

"As we go into District and Regional play, we're not playing sandlot five, but teams that have also won their league championships and into hostile environments against teams that are rough and tough---teams we've not seen before and don't know their strength or weaknesses, if any.

"For the next week of practice, I want to see serious work on play-making, shooting and footwork. We need this before our first District game and those will be played over at Ferris State College in two and a half weeks.

"If we win the District, and we will, we will move on to the court at Alma College for the Regional Championships. From there it's a short step to Lansing for the Finals."

He paused a moment and then wrapped it up with, "Now practice seriously and keep your eye always 'on the ball'."

CHAPTER 24

Interrupted by Deer Season

I'VE FISHED SEVERAL times with an old buddy I used to refer to as 'dumb old Gerald.' Well, we've also hunted together for rabbits, squirrels and even deer. And I must say that although Gerald was and is an expert fisherman, he originally lacked any knowledge of deer hunting.

The first and only time we hunted deer together was an experience for the books. Actually, it made me want to tie his shoelaces together and throw him out the cabin door into the swamp. But it sure took my mind off basketball for a tad!

Let's return to that thrilling day of yesteryear.

Gerald was a different sort of 'bloke,' and did I mention that he was a transplant from Australia? Well, he was, and he moved to Michigan with his parents from along an outback billabong when he was eleven. And since he'd already taken on the 'burl of spakin' Australian,' was sometimes, no, always, next to impossible to understand.

For several years Gerald and I attended school together, and that was when I was learning to become a hunter and fisherman, which I was to discover he already was!

Our first hunting adventure as 'mates' just happened to be a November deer hunt. Well, Gerald jumped in the car with Dad and me at six in the morning, waving about a new 12-gauge shotgun his father had purchased for him the day before. Dad gave me one of those I-told-you-so looks as he rapidly removed the gun from Gerald's grasp and stuffed it in the trunk with ours.

"Well," beamed Gerald, "Let's 'ave a go at them roos!"

"Roos?" says I, shooting him a look of disbelief. "We're not after any hopping kangaroos. Deer's what we're after."

"Hang on a tick," he replied. "What's a deer?"

I glanced at my father, who was suddenly slouched down behind the wheel with a look of impending peril on his face. So, with an inkling of an approaching disaster and a sudden view of my father tossing Gerald from a moving vehicle, I jerked my head around and faced the rear seat.

"Deer! You know. You've seen pictures of 'em in school—those animals with flashing white tails, and sometimes even with antlers!"

"Well Bob's your uncle," said a wide-eyed Gerald, "I got it. We've some of them down under too. Still, probably like huntin' roos. Guess I was away with the pixies for a tick. So deer are the dinkum we're about. Well stone the crows!"

At that point I turned back to pretend to actually notice the woods along the two-track road, thinking a nightmare was approaching.

"You boys better hunt near me this morning," Dad finally remarked with a glance in my direction. "It'll be safer for all of us that way."

It was a typical, freezing November morning with a light snow falling when Dad finally parked the car and ferreted around in the trunk for our guns and ammo. His was a 30/06 and mine a single-barrel 12-gauge similar to Gerald's. I was handed a box of slugs and turned to ask Gerald where his were.

"Well guts for garters," he exclaimed, "I'm a boofhead if I didn't leave 'em back in the dunny!"

I wasn't certain what a 'dunny' was at the time, but hastened to dig into my own shells and hand him a few.

'Don't load those guns until we're up the trail and into position," cautioned Dad as we hiked into the woods a ways. Then he pointed me over to a stump and said, "I'll take Gerald on in some and then return to where I'm between you guys." And just then I thought I caught a moment of hesitation, as though he'd had a sudden revelation of placing himself in a crossfire. Then they continued up the trail.

Anyway, I sat down on that stump and waited for daylight. It was a quiet morning thus far, and gradually getting light enough to see deer, perhaps even antlers.

A brief snow shower had somewhat ebbed when a shot rang out to my right, fairly close by. Then I heard hooves pounding in my direction and looked to see a buck with a large rack bounding right at me! And, almost unbelievably, the buck stopped about 20 yards away and turned sideways, sniffing the air.

I raised my shotgun, aimed and fired, and rather than a loud report and a slam to my shoulder, there came a subtle 'click'—I'd given Gerald some shells and forgot to load my own gun!

Of course the deer heard that click, glanced my way, and escaped at an angle to my left.

Dad was suddenly at my side. "Was that you that fired? Did you get 'im?"

I then explained what I'd done, or foolishly not done, all coming out as Dad stood there in disbelief.

And just then another shot rang out from up the hill. We looked at each other with no little amazement.

"Has to be Gerald," was all I said.

So we hurried up the hill to find 'dumb old Gerald' hovering over 'my' eight-point buck, and 'flash as a rat' there he was, decked out in rapture and a huge smile.

"Man," he says, 'that roo was comin' at me flat out like a lizard drinkin—put the wind up me for a tick! But I got 'im."

So 'dumb old Gerald' had really done it. Never mind that he didn't know a deer from a roo, or that he'd forgotten his own shells. We congratulated him anyway.

After all, Dad and I were only a couple of 'septic tanks' (Americans, if you will) while 'dumb old Gerald' was a natural-born hunter, a 'tall poppy' from way down under!

106

CHAPTER 25

The 12ᵗʰ Varsity Letter

THE CLASS D Regional Basketball finals were held at Alma College. There were only four teams in the finals and Baldwin was one of them.

We won our opening game handily on a Friday evening in November and Fowler won theirs as well. This meant we would meet Saturday evening for the Regional Championship and the right to go to the Finals in Lansing.

It was a wild game and I couldn't miss the basket and scored 29 points in the first half.

But there was a real problem for me. It appeared to me as though one referee in particular was targeting me, to get me out of that game. He used every excuse, even if I got near their point guard, George Fox, and never troubled him, to call a foul on me. The result was that I was fouled out with 5 calls in the first half, and with 29 points!

From then on we couldn't have beaten that team with five aces! Fowler won, of course, and went on to Lansing to win the Class D 1951 State Championship. We went back to Baldwin.

Soon after I received an offer from Alma College to attend there with a basketball scholarship, which I accepted. But that year I was honored with my 11th Varsity letter for Baldwin High School.

There was still one letter to go, and that was on our spring track team. The season was good to me. I won a few District and Regional medals and took 2nd place in the Michigan State running broad jump with a leap just under 20 feet. We had a good track team and medaled in several other events. Oh, who took first place in the broad jump? Well, it was my partner in all the Baldwin spots, Bill Ayers, who beat me out by one-half-of-an inch! Good for him! He took the Gold Medal and I got the Silver.

When the track season ended, I received my 12th Varsity citation from Baldwin High School. It was the end of my 4-year war and I looked forward to Alma College, but the Korean War was on and many of my buddies were already joining up....But that's another story, which is in one of my other books, "Toyoko".

* * * *

My day-long trip down "Memory Lane" was now complete, and it appeared that my mind had been fishing elsewhere than in the Pere Marquette River.

I fired up the old Ford Ranger and turned away from what had been an old "turkey patch" field and at last headed toward the river. Dusk was approaching, but perhaps I could yet get a trout to rise to one of my flies.

One thing was certain; there would be no awards for my fishing! My four-year war on competitive sports was over now and it was time to fish.

* * * *

There is one other thing I'd like to say. No matter who you are or where you are, you simply can't bring back those early years. No, not even to capture 12 Varsity letters, and they really weren't so great after all – just pieces of paper.

What I've discovered is that those high school years and awards weren't really about those letters or about my destination, but about the unforgettable experiences along the way. Those I will live over my lifetime.

THE END

Printed in the United States
By Bookmasters